A Storybook of
Ugly Ogres and
Terrible Trolls

Readers, Beware!

When you were small you probably heard stories about gruesome creatures who frightened innocent billy goats, tried to eat beanstalk-climbing boys, and lurked in the dark, ready to pounce on unwary passers-by. I'm not talking about fairies or elves. I'm not even talking about goblins, who can be tricky to deal with. No, I mean the real villains of the world of fairy tales – giants and ogres and trolls.

Well, I'm sorry to say that a lot of misleading information has been given out on this subject. Giants are big, of course, but they are as harmless as kittens – except when they try to do their own rewiring. Ogres aren't the friendliest of folk, but their cooking is out of this world – and it almost never includes small children. As for trolls, they couldn't care less about billy goats. The single thing that trolls are interested in is neither hairy nor hooved. It is yellow and shiny – gold.

If you want to find out more about the truth behind fairy tale fibs, read on. Truth, as they say, is often stranger than stories!

A Storybook of
Ugly Ogres and
Terrible Trolls

Ten Fantastic Tales of Frightful Fun

WRITTEN BY NICOLA BAXTER • ILLUSTRATED BY KEN MORTON

ARMADILLO

This edition is published by Armadillo, an imprint of Anness Publishing Ltd,
Blaby Road, Wigston, Leicestershire LE18 4SE; info@anness.com

www.annesspublishing.com

If you like the images in this book and would like to investigate using them
for publishing, promotions or advertising, please visit our website
www.practicalpictures.com for more information.

Publisher: Joanna Lorenz
Produced by Nicola Baxter
Editorial Consultant: Ronne Randall
Designer: Amanda Hawkes
Production Designer: Amy Barton
Production Controller: Pirong Wang

PUBLISHER'S NOTE
The author and publishers have made every effort to ensure that this book
is safe for its intended use, and cannot accept any legal responsibility or
liability for any harm or injury arising from misuse.

Manufacturer: Anness Publishing Ltd, Blaby Road, Wigston,
Leicestershire LE18 4SE, England
For Product Tracking go to: www.annesspublishing.com/tracking
Batch: 6714-22344-1127

Contents

Beware of the Ogre!

There are ogres who are only slightly unpleasant. They don't wash their hair (or anything else!) as often as they might. Their fingernails are long and pointy. They like to trip people and run off with their shopping bags. They are a nuisance and best avoided.

But there is another kind of ogre who is much, much more worrying. He will eat anything he finds (including cats and grandmothers). He will jump out at you when you least expect it. He is the kind of ogre your mother always warned you about.

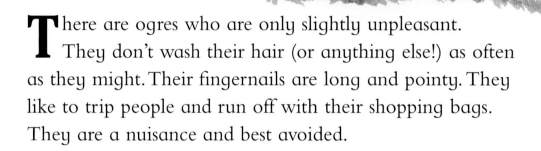

It was the second kind of ogre that lived in the dark forest near the village of Mingle, so people said. At one time, Mingle was a happy place, where elves went about their business singing and little children played outside their homes. But ever since the ogre came to live nearby, things had changed.

At night, mother elves would sing to their children:

> *Little ones,*
> *Close your eyes,*
> *Grow up happy,*
> *Healthy and wise.*
> *But never go near*
> *the forest. Beware!*
> *A horrible, terrible*
> *Ogre lives there!*

Yes, the elves of Mingle were frightened. They felt that they couldn't go into the forest for picnics any more. Worse still, they felt that they couldn't go into the forest for firewood. The first winter after the ogre arrived was a very cold one. The little elves shivered in their homes and pulled the bedclothes up to their chins.

By the time winter was almost over, the elves were miserable and too scared to set foot outside the village. Sometimes if you are very frightened, it's hard to think straight. That is exactly what had happened to the elves.

Then, one fine day, a troll came marching through the village on his way to the mines. He noticed right away that something was wrong, and although elves don't like trolls very much either, they found themselves telling him the whole story.

"We know the ogre is still there," said old Mrs Mumm, "because we can see the smoke from his fire."

"So," grunted the troll, "he's one of the worst kind, is he?"

"The very worst," said Mrs Mumm.

"Worse than worst," said Mr Pringle, her cousin.

"I don't want to open up old wounds," said the troll, "but what sort of thing has he done?"

The elves all spoke at once.

"He frightened my cow, so she wouldn't give any milk for a week!"

"He ate one of my chickens and chased the rest away!"

"He pulled up all my cabbages and half of my carrots!"

9

"And we haven't seen a single squirrel since he arrived," added Mrs Mumm darkly.

"Wait a minute. Let me get this straight," muttered the troll. "He hasn't eaten any children. He hasn't eaten any grandmothers. He hasn't even eaten any cats. He helped himself to one chicken – maybe – and some vegetables. That's bad, of course, but it's not very, very bad, is it?"

"Don't forget the squirrels," said Mrs Mumm.

"It's winter," the troll replied patiently. "All self-respecting squirrels are tucked up in their beds asleep, waiting for spring to come. I'm not saying this ogre isn't a nasty piece of work. I'm saying you don't really *know*. Why don't we try to find out?"

Mrs Mumm strode forward. "I'll do it!" she cried. "And what's more, I've got a plan."

Mrs Mumm's plan was this. She would take a large basket of food to the very edge of the forest and sit down as if to have a picnic. If the ogre came out and stole the food to eat, they would know that he was not so bad after all. If he came out and stole Mrs Mumm to eat, it would be a different story.

The troll looked at Mrs Mumm with admiration.

"It's a bit risky," he said. "Are you sure?"

"I'm going to take my knitting with me," said Mrs Mumm. "One jab with my needles and that old ogre will think twice about making a meal out of *me*!"

So Mrs Mumm filled her basket and off she went.

As many of the villagers as could manage – and the visiting troll – climbed up into the church steeple with Mr Pringle's telescope to watch what happened.

"She's sitting down by the basket," reported Mr Pringle. "Don't push, young Perkins! It's my telescope, you know!"

After that, nothing happened for a long time. Everyone got bored and started wishing they had brought sandwiches. Then, suddenly, Mr Pringle said, "Oh my goodness!" and fell down in a faint. When young Perkins took his place at the telescope, all he could see was a piece of flattened grass. No ogre. No basket. And no Mrs Mumm.

"Now what do we do?" asked Mr Pringle, when he came to. All eyes turned to the troll.

"We'd better go and find out," said the troll with a sigh. "Come on. If we all go, we can run away in lots of directions at once and confuse him."

Tottering on tiptoes, the elves and the troll crept to the edge of the forest. As they reached the first trees, Mr Pringle began to sniff the air.

"There's a wonderful smell," he said. "Is it roast chicken? Is it roast pork?"

A dreadful silence fell over the party.

"Is it roast Mrs Mumm?" asked young Perkins, who never knew when to keep quiet.

"There's only one way to find out," grunted the troll grimly. "Come on!"

13

Through the dark trees the trembling troop stumbled, growing closer and closer to the smell of something truly delicious. Then, through the trees, they saw an amazing sight.

In a clearing where a huge pot was bubbling over a fire, the ogre and old Mrs Mumm were sitting comfortably, nibbling a variety of delicate *hors d'oeuvres*. They appeared to be discussing the finer points of pastry-making.

"Ah, there you are!" cried Mrs Mumm, when she saw the peeping party. "Meet my friend Horgrish!"

Horgrish was no Prince Charming. His table manners were dreadful. But he was ferociously interested in food and could cook like a dream. Even the wariest elves found their feet mysteriously drawn toward the steaming bowls that the ogre was (rather untidily) filling.

That afternoon, the elves learned three things. It's a mistake to judge by appearances. Cool hands are needed for making pastry. And a finely seasoned vegetable stew, eaten in the open air in good company, can more than make up for even the most miserable winter.

The Ugliest Ogre Contest

All ogres are ugly. They are proud of it. If you tell a young ogre that his mother looks like a toad, he won't smack you on the head with a smelly fish or throw you in a puddle and jump up and down on your middle. He will probably go pink with pleasure and say, "Oh, thanks!"

On the other hand, when a mother ogre shows you her new baby, it's a big mistake to say, "Ooooh! Cootchy, cootchy coo! Isn't he handsome?" You might well find yourself upside down in an ogre-sized bowl of toad-spawn soup.

You will begin to see, now, why the annual Ugliest Ogre Contest was a big event. Ogres, as you know, have a bad reputation with most elves, and one ogre in the area was more than enough. But the annual Ugliest Ogre Contest was held in a different part of the country each year. Each summer, somewhere in Elfland, one unlucky bunch of elves, going about their business with not a care in the world, was about to be visited by not one, not two, but hundreds of ogres. This year it was the town of Umble that drew the short straw.

The first the elves of Umble knew about the Ugliest Ogre Contest was when old Ma Placket, doing her laundry early one Monday morning, was suddenly terrified out of her wits by a grinning face at the window. It turned her blood cold and her washing green. Much to the relief of old Pa Placket, she was unable to speak for days.

Ma Placket may have been silent, but she pretty soon made sure that everyone knew there were ogres on the loose. By lunchtime, every house had its shutters drawn and its doors barred. No elves stirred on the streets of Umble, but several hundred ogres clomped heavily over the cobblestones with just one thought on their minds: ugliness.

Now ogres are not very competitive. When it comes to running, jumping or throwing anything larger than a pork pie they couldn't care less who is fastest, highest, or hungriest. But when the subject is ugliness, they care very much indeed. All year, the main contenders in the contest had been undergoing rigorous ugliness regimes, aimed at heightening their hideousness.

"They say," an ogre called Glurp told his friend, "that Aaghish George puts a poultice of hedgehog spikes and nettles on his face every day."

"That's nothing," replied Plurk. "Burple Punkt never washes, never combs his hair, and never cuts his nails. My sister thinks he's soooo ugly, she has a picture of him on her wall."

The details of the contest would have horrified the orderly little elves who were still crouching in their houses. You see, ogres are suspicious of anyone telling them what to do. That is why there is no ogre king, or prime minister, or president. They prefer to shamble along in an untidy sort of way, getting what they want mainly by shouting and shaking their fists. It's not that they actually ever come to blows, but a shaking fist is an ugly thing, which is just what ogres like.

So it will not surprise you to know that Ugliest Ogre Contests do not have proper judges or referees with score cards. Instead, members of the audience yell for the ogre they personally find unbelievably unbeautiful. It is a horrible noise and it sometimes goes on for days.

In the meantime, the contestants try to make the ugliest faces they can, which is exhausting. It's as difficult to frown all the time as it is to smile all the time, and some ogre smiles, I fear, are more hideous than any other ogre expression. Anything that shows pointy yellow teeth can't be good, you must admit.

On the day of the contest itself, the ogres gathered in the town square. To get a good view, some of them sat on nearby rooftops, doing serious damage to chimneys in the process. In the middle of the square, on a specially built stage, the contestants strutted their stuff.

First to appear was Aaghish George. "Ugly" doesn't really begin to express the awfulness of his face. One glimpse of it would make you lose your appetite for a month. Two glimpses might finish you off altogether. But the ogres loved it. Admiring murmurs arose from the crowd. Several female ogres fainted. Aaghish George was going to be hard to beat.

But Burple Punkt had a horribleness of features that was quite ghastly. The ogres roared their approval. Burple held his breath until his face turned purple and his eyes almost popped out. The crowd loved it.

There were a few other contestants, of course, but it soon became clear that this was a two-ogre race. Aaghish George and Burple Punkt were the only ones in with a chance. They glared at each other and wiggled their ears.

21

"The mirror test! The mirror test!" yelled the crowd. It was a well-known ploy at times like this. Sure enough, several elf shops were raided and the large plate-glass mirrors inside were dragged out.

"Ready, steady, go!" chanted the crowd. At just the same moment, mirrors were raised in front of Aaghish George's and Burple Punkt's faces. Immediately, the mirrors smashed into tiny fragments. The ugliness was simply too much for them. The test was a dead heat.

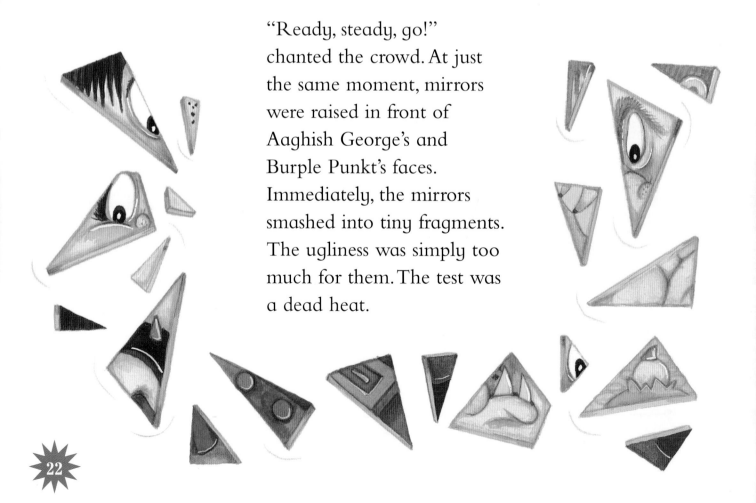

Now the watching ogres were yelling so hard they were becoming hoarse.

"Aaghish George! A-a-g-h-i-s-h G-e-o-r-g-e!" shouted one side of the square.

"Burple Punkt! B-u-r-p-l-e P-u-n-k-t!" shouted the other.

"I can't stand this any more," said Ma Placket, barricaded in her kitchen with Pa Placket and her sister's cow. "The sooner this is over, the better. We'll have to get rid of one of the contestants. Then the other will be the clear winner, the ogres will go home, and we can live normal lives again. What we need is a plan."

But as it turned out, Ma Placket didn't need a plan. Five ogres, eager to shout and cheer more loudly decided that the rooftops were not tall enough. Eagerly and clumsily, they began to climb the church steeple – the same church steeple that an elvish engineer had recently shaken his head over.

23

There was an ominous rumbling. There was an even more ominous clanging from the big bell in the belfry. The crowd of ogres looked up and screamed. The steeple swayed … and fell … *crash!* … onto the heads of Aaghish George and his great rival.

When the dust cleared, the two contestants lay still. There was silence from the crowd. Then a sigh of relief ran through the crowd as first Aaghish George and then Burple Punkt rose from the wreckage.

But the sighs of relief soon turned to sighs of horror. Aaghish George, covered with dirt and twigs and with a weather vane perched on his head, looked uglier than ever. But Burple Punkt had something different on his head – the bell!

It covered his face completely. You couldn't have said he looked beautiful. You couldn't have said he was attractive in any way. But you couldn't have said he was ugly either.

Burple Punkt pulled and tugged. Some extremely ogreish language, unfit for the ears of young elves, came booming out of the bell, but that was all. No face appeared. He was stuck.

There was no doubt about it. Aaghish George was clearly the ugliest ogre present. To the cheers of his supporters, he was carried shoulder-high from the square and out of the town. Poor Burple Punkt, still booming, was led away as well.

One by one, the elves of Umble crawled out of their homes and viewed the state of their square. It looked awful. But let's face it, compared with dozens of truly hideous ogres, it was absolutely, overwhelmingly … *gorgeous!*

A Home for an Ogre

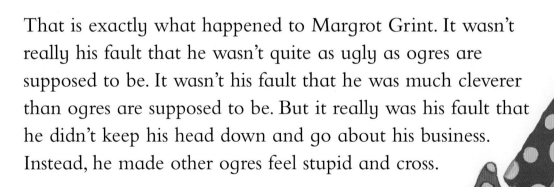

Now you don't need me to tell you that ogres are not the most popular visitors to Elfland villages. In fact, the only people who really like ogres are ogres themselves. And that is why, if an ogre falls out with his own family and friends, he is in very big trouble indeed.

That is exactly what happened to Margrot Grint. It wasn't really his fault that he wasn't quite as ugly as ogres are supposed to be. It wasn't his fault that he was much cleverer than ogres are supposed to be. But it really was his fault that he didn't keep his head down and go about his business. Instead, he made other ogres feel stupid and cross.

One fine summer's evening, for example, Margrot and some
other ogres were sitting outside gazing at the stars. Even ogres
have their poetic moments.

"It's amazing," said Mr Mung, the schoolteacher. "They are
so far away that no one knows exactly how far they are."
"Oh yes they do," said Margrot bluntly. And he
proceeded to give the whole company a lecture
on astrophysics. The others didn't understand
one word of it, but they couldn't help feeling
that the mood of the evening had been spoiled.

It was the same when Margrot came across his old granny making ugly cakes. Now Margrot's old granny had been making ugly cakes for almost two hundred years (yes, ogres really do live that long). When her grandson began to tell her that she needed the oven to be hotter and the mixture to be colder, she didn't take kindly to his advice. The fact that he was absolutely right – and she knew it – only made matters worse.

After several years of not having the sense to keep his mouth shut, Margrot found that most ogres crossed the street when they saw him coming. Then his landlord told him that he would have to move out of his little cottage.

"It's out of my hands," said the landlord. "I'm sorry, but you'll have to go."

In vain, Margrot tried to find out what on earth he meant.
The landlord turned his back and said that he would be
changing the locks on Friday.

Margrot searched the whole
village for a new home, but
there was nothing to be had.
Even his nearest and dearest
seemed strangely reluctant to
ask him to stay. When
Friday came, Margrot found
himself standing outside his
old home with a bag of
dirty clothes (ogres are no
better at washing their
clothes than they are at
washing themselves) and
four large volumes of tried
and tested recipes. With a
sigh that made the buds on
a nearby rosebush shrivel,
he set off to find another
place to live.

It wasn't easy. Banished by his own kind, Margrot Grint soon
found that he was even more disliked by the elves who lived
nearby. The ones that didn't scream and run away when they
saw him fell down in a faint instead. None of them greeted
him warmly and asked him to move into a spare bedroom.

So it was that Margrot, like many ogres before him, set up home in the forest. It was cold in winter, full of stinging insects in summer, and the bathroom facilities left a lot to be desired. And Margrot was lonely. Even the local elves never ventured into the forest now that they knew Someone Else had taken up residence there.

But one day, as Margrot rested in the treehouse he had built in an enormous oak, he heard the sound of crying below. It was a small elfin boy, wailing and thumping a spelling book at the same time.

"What's the matter?" called Margrot. "Can I help?"

The boy jumped. "Only if you can do level nine elf spelling," he moaned. He couldn't see Margrot through the leaves, so he didn't know he was talking to an ogre.

Margrot Grint was so pleased to talk to another living soul that he did a sensible thing. He stayed in his treehouse and talked the boy through his problems without showing himself. After half an hour of careful coaching, the boy suddenly understood a lot more about spelling than he ever had before. He ran back to his village with a smug little grin.

It wasn't long before news of the "Wise Man of the Forest" spread among the elf children. Margrot found himself helping out with the homework of every child in the village. He enjoyed it – but never

came down into the open.
Very, very slowly, grown-up
elves also began to come for
advice. Margrot gave his
opinion on problems with
relatives (after all, he knew
all about that), composting
methods (ogres are skilled at
anything to do with
smelliness), bread baking,
basketweaving and babycare.
He found that cleverness and
common sense could come
up with an answer to almost
any problem.

Pretty soon, no one did
anything without consulting
the Wise Man first. Most
mornings, an orderly line
wound among the trees,
waiting to speak to the voice
in the tree.

Gradually, summer changed
to autumn. The leaves
started to fall.

Margrot began to worry.

The day came at last, as he knew it would, when an autumn gale, howling through the treetops, swept the last leaves from his tree. Looking up, a member of the crowd below caught a glimpse of Margrot Grint … and screamed.

Margrot had no choice. He clambered down and prepared to be rejected.

"Yes," he said, "I am an ogre. Now, I suppose, you will all run away."

But elves, unlike most ogres, are not stupid. Margrot was a very useful person to know.

"Ah, yes, hello Mr Ogre," said the elves' mayor. "Now, about my plumbing…."

Giant Jim's Joke

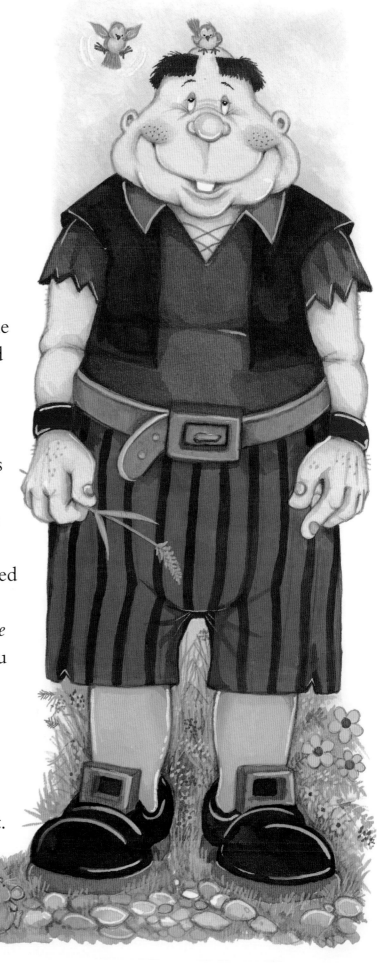

There are times when the very best kind of friend to have is a giant. If your car is stuck in the mud, he will happily pull it out for you. If your chimney needs repairs, he will cheerfully hold you up at roof-height while you fix it. (Don't, whatever you do, be tempted to let a giant do the fixing himself. His fingers are *large* but they are not *delicate*. You could end up with more damage than you started with.) Yes, a giant can be very good at some things, but hopeless at others – as young Elbert Elf found out.

Elbert first made friends with Giant Jim when, as quite a small elf, he dropped his best red-and-blue ball into Lillimug Lake and it floated out of reach. Elbert was just about to start weeping and wailing when the ground around him began to shake. The fate of one red-and-blue ball didn't seem so important when the ground became as wobbly as jelly.

"What's the trouble, little chap?" boomed a voice that seemed to come out of the sky.

Elbert looked up … and up … and up … and up. Far, far above him, a friendly face beamed down.

"My name is Jim," it went on. "Shall I fetch your ball for you?"

Elbert was too surprised even to nod, but the giant waded into the lake – the water only came up to his ankles – and picked up the ball as if it was a pea.

After that, the giant and the little elf became great friends. Elbert soon realized there was no need to be afraid of the giant. He was always very careful where he put his big feet when little ones were around. What Elbert liked best was to ride around on Jim's shoulders. It was almost as good as being a giant himself.

But as Elbert grew older, he began to find some things about his friend annoying.

The main reason was that Jim, like most giants, really wasn't very clever. That didn't matter most of the time. Elbert didn't need help with his history homework – he could do that himself. But Elbert loved jokes, and he found that his giant friend simply didn't get them.

"What lies at the bottom of the sea and shivers, Jim?" asked the young elf.

"I don't know," replied Jim.

"A nervous wreck!" chortled Elbert.

"What was it nervous about?" asked Jim.

"No, no, it was a joke," Elbert tried to explain, but it was no use. In fact, if you've ever tried it, you'll know that it's pretty hard to explain why a joke is funny. It just is, somehow.

Elbert thought he might be able to *teach* Jim to understand jokes. He spent a lot of time explaining to him how "Knock! Knock!" jokes work. At last, he thought Jim had got it.

One day, Elbert asked Jim. "Will you remember me tomorrow?"

"Of course I will, Elbert," said Jim.

"Will you remember me in a week?"

"Of course," said Jim.

"Will you remember me in a year?"

"I'm sure I will," said Jim, "but you're not going anywhere, are you, Elbert?"

"Knock! Knock!" said Elbert.

Jim felt on safer ground. "Who's there?" he bellowed.

"See!" laughed the elf. "You've forgotten me already!"

"It was a *joke*, Jim," sighed Elbert. "But you never get them, do you? Maybe we just don't have enough in common to be best friends."

Elbert went off by himself and decided not to spend so much time with Jim. The giant lumbered back to his castle and wished he had never met the little elf. But both of them were miserable. Elbert found himself spending most of his time trying to think of a way of making everything right with his giant friend.

But in the end, it was Jim who broke the ice. One morning, as Elbert was leafing sadly through his jokebook, which suddenly didn't seem so very funny, there came a hammering at the door.

"There's only one person *that* could be," said Elbert's mother. "How that door stays on its hinges I'll never know."

Elbert hurried to the door. He could never ask his friend inside, for the roof of the little house only came up to the giant's knees. Outside the door was a pair of familiar legs – but something was odd.

"Jim," shouted Elbert, "you've got your shoes on the
wrong feet!"

"But these are the only feet I've got!" replied Jim.

"That's not what I mean…" Elbert began, but Jim was
roaring with laughter and making the windows wobble.

"It was a *joke*, Elbert!" he cried. "It was a *joke*!"

For a moment, Elbert's heart lifted. Jim had got it! He would
be able to share his funniest jokes with him! But he soon
found out he was wrong. Poor old Jim had found *one* joke
that he understood. He had been rehearsing for a week to get
it right (and he had driven most of his friends and relations
mad in the process). It had been hard work for him, but he
had done it to please his friend.

Elbert smiled sadly at his jokebook.
Somehow, he had missed Jim more
than his jokes. And, after all, one
joke a year was better
than nothing.

No Giants Allowed!

Most of the time, elves are easy-going little people who don't worry too much about what anybody else is doing. It's true that they're not particularly fond of ogres, and they're a little wary of trolls as well, but elves are usually prepared to give them the benefit of the doubt.

Giants are a different matter. Everyone likes giants. They are friendly and try to be helpful. But no one can deny that giants are *big*, and in the eyes of elves, big isn't necessarily beautiful.

The whole matter came out into the open when Everlettle Emble agreed to marry Engers Eartwist.

They were both elves, so, of course, they planned an elfin wedding. You know the sort of thing: lots of rose petals and garlands, elderflower wine in acorn cups, and a dress for Everlettle made from daisies and dew-drops with a veil of cobweb lace.

It was Everlettle's mother who forced her to sit down one day and finish her guest list. Elves like to invite all their friends and relations to their weddings – even fourth cousins fifteen times removed and people they once bumped bags with at a busy market.

It was not surprising, then, that it took Everlettle hours and hours to complete her huge list. It was late at night and she was working by the light of a firefly lantern by the end.

Everlettle's mother was half asleep when she finally got her hands on the list, but a bride's mother has to have her wits about her. Sleepy Everlettle was roused by her mother's sharp little scream.

"*Everlettle!* What's this? Jerry Jagglethorpe? That isn't any elfin name, surely? It almost sounds like, well, I can hardly say it. It almost sounds like a *giant's* name."

"I don't know," yawned Everlettle, looking over her mother's shoulder. "It's one of Engers's friends. You'll have to ask him."

"I certainly will," said Mrs Emble. First thing in the morning, she was knocking on Engers's door, with the list trailing behind her.

Engers was as helpful as could be. "Yes, old Jerry Jagglethorpe
is a giant," he said cheerfully. "Dear old Jerry! I grew up with
him and had some of my jolliest times tramping around with
him. Giants are such friendly chaps, aren't they?"

Mrs Emble paused and considered how to address the matter
delicately. "They are friendly," she said at last, "and in most
circumstances I would say they are fine folk. A little simple in
their ideas, perhaps, but none the worse for that. But…"

Engers waited. "But…?" he prompted.

"But they are a disaster at
weddings," said Mrs Emble
firmly. "Imagine what would
happen to our garlands and
cobweb lace if a giant put
his great foot on them. Even
a cough or, goodness me, a
sneeze could spell disaster.
Giants' sneezes are
like tornadoes."

"Well, that's true," Engers admitted, remembering a time when he ended up in the river because Jerry had hiccups. "But really, he is my oldest friend. I can't *not* invite him."

"You can … you can't … oh, you know what I mean," said Mrs Emble with some firmness. "I would go so far as to say, young Engers, that there will be no wedding if Jerry Jagglethorpe puts his big boots within five miles of Everlettle's special day. And I'm talking giant miles, not elfin ones. Do you understand me?"

Engers did. He was very fond of Jerry, but he loved his Everlettle even more. He planned to write a friendly letter to the giant explaining everything, but somehow, with all the wedding plans to take care of, he forgot.

Elfin weddings, of course, are held outdoors. With so many elves invited, there is nowhere big enough to contain them all inside. Obviously, good weather is very important. Elves are very clever about the weather. They use all kinds of little signs to predict when it will be sunny and fine. The way that earwigs wiggle, the size of chestnut leaves, and the texture of the bark of the birch trees are all important.

It was only after consulting Esperance Extreel, the best weathermonger in Elfland, that the date of Everlettle's wedding was set.

But even elfin weathermongers make mistakes. Everlettle's wedding was in full swing when Mrs Emble, supervising the serving of the elderflower wine, looked up and saw two disasters approaching her daughter's special moment at horrifying speed. One was the biggest, blackest storm cloud you have ever seen. The other was Giant Jerry Jagglethorpe, in his best suit and with his boots polished. Mrs Emble fainted.

It was, perhaps, unfortunate that most elves assumed that the mother of the bride needed to lie down for a while after too much elderflower wine. By the time Mrs Emble staggered to her feet again, the storm cloud was right overhead and Jerry Jagglethorpe was about to place his shiny boots horribly close to the table with the wedding cake on it.

Mrs Emble could not make herself heard above the music and laughter. Without a thought for her finery, she scrambled up the nearest oak tree and clambered to the top. There, popping her head out from among the leaves, she found herself nose to nose with Jerry Jagglethorpe.

"Hello!" he boomed, making branches sway dangerously. "I think my invitation must have got lost."

"Please," yelled Mrs Emble, clinging on for dear life. "GO AWAY!"

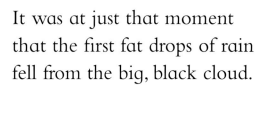

It was at just that moment that the first fat drops of rain fell from the big, black cloud.

"Oh no!" wailed Mrs Emble.

"Oh, I see!" thundered Jerry Jagglethorpe. "You want me to make this old cloud GO AWAY!" He filled his cheeks like balloons and *blew* with all his might. The big, black cloud zoomed away towards the mountains, where it put an end to a terribly exciting game of ogreball – but that is another story.

Mrs Emble took a deep breath. She was firm but she was fair. "Please," she said, smiling at the giant, "come and join us."

So it was that *all* Engers's and Everlettle's friends were with them on the first of the many, many happy days they shared.

The Gentle Giant

You may remember the story of Everlettle's and Engers's wedding. It was certainly talked about for many years in elfin circles. Well, the couple were very happy together and everyone was delighted when they found they were expecting their first baby. Only they weren't. Expecting their first baby, that is. It turned out that they were expecting their first, second and third babies – all at once.

Triplets are about as rare among elves as they are among human folk. When Everlettle's babies finally put in an appearance, the news ran around Elfland like wildfire. They were all girls, with little pink faces and sweet pointy ears. Dozens of elves, especially old lady elves, lined up to coo over the little ones.

But Everlettle's daughters were not the little angels that their visitors assumed. As soon as the door was shut and only Everlettle was left to look after them, they opened their little mouths, screwed up their little eyes, and *yelled*. Feeding didn't stop them. Funny faces didn't stop them. The only thing they really liked was being rocked in Everlettle's arms.

Poor Everlettle! She had three babies. She had two arms. No matter how hard she tried, she could not jiggle three babies up and down at once. By the time Engers came home from working in the fields, she was desperate.

Engers, who had not been at home with three screaming babies all day, was able to think a little more clearly. He decided that some kind of automatic rocking machine was the answer to all their problems.

"Couldn't you take one of them?" begged Everlettle. But Engers was already halfway to his workshop.

Engers was a clever elf but he had little experience of making automatic rocking machines. His first effort was downright dangerous. When he sat a cushion in it to test it, the cushion went flying up into the treetops and is probably still there. Although Engers's next try was better, it did take a long time to make improvements to it. Engers kept working on.

Meanwhile, in the house, Everlettle had coped with three screaming babies for what seemed like hundreds of years.

Finally, she wrenched open the workshop door and screamed a few well-chosen words at her husband. It was just at this moment that Jerry Jagglethorpe, Engers's giant friend, arrived to visit the babies. Of course, they stopped crying at once.

Jerry usually thought pretty slowly, but he wasn't stupid. He soon realized that all was not well. When the parents explained that they had had no sleep for ages and that it was impossible to stop the babies crying, he offered to help at once.

Everlettle looked at Jerry's giant hands. It was impossible that he could pick up a tiny baby without squashing or squidging her. Engers helped his wife to explain why they didn't think it was a good idea for the giant to hold the little ones. Jerry looked sad.

Just then, the giant noticed Engers's various rocking machine models. When they weren't moving, they simply looked like cradles with handles.

"I've had an idea," said Jerry Jagglethorpe (which was not something that happened very often!).

The giant carefully tied three cradles to the lowest branch of a nearby tree. Then he asked Everlettle to lay the babies in the cradles.

"I don't think this is going to work," said Engers gently. "The tree only sways a little bit – not enough to make the babies go to sleep."

But Jerry paid no attention. He lay down on the ground under the cradles and closed his eyes. Soon, to the tired parents' astonishment, the giant was fast asleep – and snoring! As he breathed noisily in and out, the cradles above his head rocked backwards and forwards, and the babies fell asleep, too. Engers and Everlettle smiled. At any other time, a giant's snores would have been extremely annoying. Today, they sounded like the most beautiful music in the world.

Gently covering Jerry with half a dozen blankets and quilts, Everlettle and Engers crept inside for a little sleep of their own. And the babies, blissfully rocking, slept until morning.

So next time you come across a giant sleeping under a tree, think twice – or even three times – before you wake him!

The Troll and the Billy Goats

Once upon a time, there were three billy goats who loved to eat fresh, green grass. Does this sound familiar? You probably already know the story of the three billy goats Gruff. At least, you know the story the *billy goats* told. The poor old troll, floating off down the river, never got a chance to tell his side of the tale.

Now, this is what really happened. Trolls, as you know, are usually only interested in one thing – gold. They spend all day long digging in the earth, or wading in streams, trying to find gleaming nuggets of the precious metal.

Even if a troll has piles and piles of gold stored in a cave somewhere (and some of them do), he never feels he has enough. He carries on digging until the end of his days.

The troll in this story was just like that. He spent his life panning for gold in the mountain streams. One sunny day, when he was working away near an old wooden bridge, he suddenly saw something glittering in the sand at the bottom of his pan. It was gold!

Chortling with glee, the troll held the pan up high and let the sunlight sparkle on his find.

Just at that moment… *Trip trap! Trip trap! Trip trap!*

A tiny billy goat came stomping over the bridge, making an incredible amount of noise with his tiny hoofs. Startled by the noise, the troll dropped his pan – and the gold that was in it – right back into the river.

Not surprisingly, he gave a howl of rage. And the tiny billy goat, thinking this sounded very much like a creature who might want to eat something small and furry, scuttled off to the other side of the bridge.

The troll grunted and growled. He had never eaten a goat in his life and didn't intend to start now, but he certainly didn't feel very friendly towards anything with horns and a silly white beard.

After a few moments, the troll's mind went back to what was really important to him. You know what *that* was. Patiently, he retrieved his pan and started dipping it into the stream once more.

He was unbelievably lucky. Once again, something gleamed at the bottom. With a crow of delight, the troll peered at the glittering gold. This time he was taking no chances. Very, very carefully, he swooshed away the sand and grit. Then he tipped the tiny grains of gold into a leather purse he kept in his pocket for just this purpose.

But just at that moment… *Trip trap! Trip trap! Trip trap!*

The middle-sized billy goat Gruff came galloping across the bridge, making a dreadful din.

59

The troll dropped his purse. It went *plop!* into the water and disappeared. This time the troll was not so restrained. He gave a huge bellow and thrust his head over the edge of the bridge, frightening the middle-sized billy goat a great deal. The creature dashed off over the bridge, convinced that a monster was about to gobble him up whole.

The poor old troll stuck his head under the water and looked about for the purse. It was a brownish shade, very much like the rocks in the stream. Every so often he came up for air, his face red and dripping.

When the troll's gnarled fingers closed around the bag at last, he breathed a sigh of relief, forgetting he was underwater. Streams of bubbles made him cough and splutter. He reared up into the air, with water streaming from him, looking quite horrifying.

In one swift movement, the troll heaved himself up onto the bridge – just as the largest billy goat Gruff came thundering across it. *Trip trap!* *TRIP TRAP!* *TRIP TRAP!*

Woomph! The billy goat wasn't looking where he was going. Quite by accident, his horns made contact with the poor old troll. He'd already had a hard day. Now he flew up into the air and landed with a mighty splash in the water. Unable to find his feet, he floated off down the stream, shrieking and waving his fists. (Yes, he had lost the purse of gold *again*.)

The billy goat was dazed by the collision. Seeing something brown and plump lying on the bridge, he promptly ate it.

So next time you are told the story of the three billy goats Gruff, don't believe everything you hear. And next time you are walking over a wooden bridge, please do it very, very *quietly*.

Troll Trouble

Trolls and elves usually don't have much to do with each other. They have very little in common. Trolls think that there is really only one truly beautiful thing in the world – gold. Elves say, "But what about rainbows? What about dew on daisies? What about butterfly wings?" Trolls think this is fanciful nonsense … and snort.

Certainly Edgerley Elf had never had anything to do with trolls before he met Tuggle. It happened like this…

Edgerley lived with his ancient great-uncle until the old elf died. Then, at last, Edgerley felt able to move to a bright, new house. He had never liked the dark little cottage under the hawthorn hedge.

Edgerley's new home was his pride and joy. It was beneath the graceful branches of a silver birch tree. Light streamed in through the windows and gleamed on Edgerley's finely polished furniture and fetching flower arrangements. The young elf was very happy.

Then, one morning, as Edgerley sat eating his supper, he heard a strange drumming sound. It seemed to be coming from under his feet. The elf assumed that a passing burrowing bunny was making more noise than usual. He hoped she wouldn't nibble too many tree roots as she went.

Next morning, however, the noise was worse. It sounded more like clanging than thudding now. Edgerley tried not to notice.

When, the following morning, Edgerley's cutlery started to jump up and down on the table, he became seriously concerned. And just as he was frowning into his buttercup tea, a great clod of earth bounced off his shoulder. A second later, a dark and dirty head and shoulders heaved itself up through the floor!

Edgerley was speechless, but the stranger wasn't. "Who," he cried, "had the idiotic idea of putting a house here?"

Edgerley found his voice. "What are you talking about? Why are you digging under my house?" he yelled.

The elf could see now that it was a troll glaring at him through the grime.

"I'm digging for gold, of course," said the troll in withering tones. "What else would I be doing? Gold is the only thing worth anything at all."

Edgerley sensed that it wasn't worth starting on the "What about rainbows?" conversation. Instead, he ordered the troll to leave at once.

The troll, whose name was Tuggle, refused. For most of the rest of the morning, the argument raged back and forth.

"A troll never gives up when he smells gold," said Tuggle. "And I smell gold right here." He sniffed the air with gruesome glee. "The sooner I can get back to work," he went on, "the sooner I'll be out of your way."

Edgerley thought for a moment. Perhaps there was something in what the troll said. Reluctantly, he agreed.

"Hurry up!" he said. "And don't make too much mess!"

Even Edgerley was impressed by how hard the troll worked. It seemed only fair to give him a drink and some sandwiches at lunchtime.

As the afternoon wore on, Edgerley found himself peering down into the ever-widening hole. It was fascinating seeing all the tree roots, creepy-crawlies and other bits and pieces under the earth. He even began to get a little bit interested in gold.

For the troll talked as he dug, and the way he spoke about the yellow metal made it sound like the most wonderful thing in the world. As night fell, Edgerley lit lanterns so that work could continue. By six o'clock he was down in the hole as well, digging away with his own little spade.

By two o'clock in the morning, the elf was as dirty and tired as the troll, but neither of them stopped. When the elf spotted a glint of something in the lamplight, his cry of triumph was just as loud as Tuggle's.

The warm sun rose over Tuggle and Edgerley sitting on the elf's doorstep, sipping buttercup tea and gazing rapturously at a chunk of gold lying on the grass before them.

"I could always use an assistant," said Tuggle.

Edgerley was about to agree when he noticed that the sun was gleaming just as richly on a little patch of buttercups by his door. He looked up at the rosy sky and sighed.

"No," he said, "I'll stay here. But thank you for asking. And good luck!"

After all, the best thing is that there is room in the wide world for both trolls and elves. If there is a pot of gold at the end of every rainbow, maybe there's a rainbow above every pot of gold.

Treasure for a Troll

When a young troll is growing up, he learns a lot about gold and how to find it. Naturally, he learns other things too: how to put lighting in the long, dark passages of gold mines, how to make a simple pair of gold-weighing scales from two twigs and a spider's web, how to stifle shouts of glee so that other trolls don't know you just found the largest nugget in the known universe.

Now, most trolls expect to work hard for their gold. They will happily dig all day and night if they feel they are in a hopeful spot. But there was once a troll who wasn't like that. His name was Trudge.

Trudge was lazy. Early in his life, it occurred to him that it was better to let someone else do all the hard work. The more Trudge lounged about not doing things, the more unfit and unenergetic he became. He couldn't have lifted a heavy shovel if he had wanted to.

He didn't want to. Trudge read books about gold and wondered what all the fuss was about. Why on earth did perfectly sensible trolls spend all their time digging in the cold, dark earth and splashing in cold, wet rivers? There was lots of gold around that had already been mined. What could possibly be wrong with helping yourself to some of that?

In the nearby elfin village of Earwax, for example, there was
a very attractive little jewel shop. Trudge began lurking
around its windows whenever he could escape from school.

It wasn't long before Mr Eardangles, the shopkeeper, became
suspicious. He peered out at the young troll and waved him
away. It is unheard of for a troll to go into a shop and buy
gold. Mr Eardangles was sure Trudge was up to no good.

He was right, of course.
Trudge viewed the racks of
rings and bracelets, the
stands of necklaces and
watches, and the many kinds
of brooches and earrings
with increasing interest. They
were yellow and shiny – just
what a troll loves.

Trudge began to plan a midnight raid on the jewel shop. It didn't seem wrong to him in any way. He liked gold. Mr Eardangles had gold. It was obvious that a transfer of the metal in question was necessary.

Sadly, Trudge's laziness was not just where gold was concerned. He never could be bothered to pay attention at school. Although the words "This shop has a very loud burglar alarm!" were written in tiny elfin writing on the shop window, Trudge was bad at foreign languages and couldn't read them. He made his preparations without this useful piece of information.

It was late one Tuesday night that Trudge crept out of his parents' house and set off for Mr Eardangles' shop.

The night was very dark, but Trudge had not thought of bringing a lantern. As a result, he walked into several trees and arrived in Earwax in an even more confused state than usual.

The bad young troll had thought about locked doors and what to do about them, but he had no real plan. He needn't have worried. Elves are small creatures and trolls – especially large young lads like Trudge – are not. The troll simply leaned heavily against the door as he tried to open it and found there was no problem at all. The elfin lock gave way under the strain, and Trudge stumbled into the dark shop.

At once, a noise like an entire brass band dropping its instruments into a cement mixer thundered out across the sleepy town of Earwax. Trudge almost jumped out of his skin, hit his head on the ceiling and sat down very suddenly on the floor. It was here that a furious Mr Eardangles found him when he rushed in five minutes later in his nightshirt.

Mr Eardangles was not the only person to arrive. Several other elves came running from their beds to see what was happening. Holding flashlights and lanterns, they peered down at the dazed young troll.

"Don't worry," said Mr Eardangles grimly. "You can all go home. Nothing has been stolen, and I can deal with this young noodle myself."

The old elf sat down on the floor next to Trudge and explained to him in clear terms why it was a complete waste of time for him ever to consider burglary again.

"I don't leave the stock out at night, you know," he said. "It is all locked away in the safe, which would take a much cleverer young troll than you to open. I'm going to take you straight home to your parents. Don't let me see you leering at the gold in my windows again."

"I wasn't leering at all of it," said Trudge, as if that made any difference. "Anyway, it's not all gold."

"What isn't?" demanded the shopkeeper. "Of course it is!"

"There are two necklaces and three bracelets that definitely aren't gold," pouted the troll.

"That's ridiculous," cried Mr Eardangles. "Anyway, how would *you* know?"

"I'm a troll," said Trudge simply.

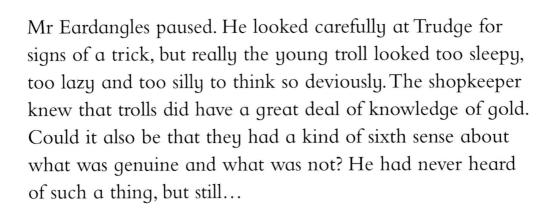

Mr Eardangles paused. He looked carefully at Trudge for signs of a trick, but really the young troll looked too sleepy, too lazy and too silly to think so deviously. The shopkeeper knew that trolls did have a great deal of knowledge of gold. Could it also be that they had a kind of sixth sense about what was genuine and what was not? He had never heard of such a thing, but still…

Telling Trudge to stay exactly where he was, Mr Eardangles went into the back room of his shop and opened his safe.

He chose one or two items from the safe and brought them
out to his uninvited guest.

"Tell me about these," he said.

To the shopkeeper's amazement, Trudge named the places
where the gold had been mined, its purity and even its value.
He also pointed to a necklace and said, "The necklace itself is
fine, but, you know, the clasp is a cheap one." He was right.

So began one of the oddest
working partnerships
between an elf and a troll
that has ever been known.
Trudge left school and
happily spent all day in Mr
Eardangles' shop, surrounded
by the metal he loved without
having to pick up a single
shovel. The shopkeeper, on
the other hand, had an
expert by his side at all times
and a possible thief never out
of his sight.

You see, just when he thinks
he knows everything there is
to know about trolls, even an
elf can be surprised.

The Party
That Shook
the World

Trolls and ogres are just like the rest of us. They have relatives – lovely ones and … well, unlovely ones. They have friends, too, although, as you know, both trolls and ogres can be fairly quarrelsome and difficult to get along with. On the whole, however, trolls and ogres are not like elves, who will throw a party just because it's Tuesday.

Giants are another matter. They just love to have people around them. A lonely giant is a very unhappy giant. So it was no surprise to anyone in the nearby elf-town of Littleham when Giant Jeremiah decided to hold a party.

"There will be music and dancing and balloons and pretty lights and lots of lovely things to eat and drink," he told his elfin friends. "I'm going to ask just a few of my very best friends – four other giants and lots of elves, of course. It will be quite a small affair."

The elves nodded, but they were worried.

"He can't cook, you know," said Mrs Migglewell. "The food will be awful."

"Have you heard his idea of music?" Asked Elvis Medley, a famous elfin singer.

"Four giants dancing is a frightening prospect," muttered old Mr Elder. "I'm thinking of the young ones."

The older elves nodded their heads and shuddered. "I'm worried about the pretty lights, too," said one. "Remember what happened when he tried to rewire his castle?"

"We're going to have to do something," said Mrs Migglewell. "If he is left to organize this by himself, it will be a disaster and very dangerous. I'll go to see him."

When the busy elf returned from Giant Jeremiah's castle, she had ominous news.

"It's going to be a bigger party than we thought, in more ways than one," she said. "Apparently, all Jeremiah's relatives from the Goblin Hills are coming. There are dozens of them!"

"We can't cook for dozens of giants!" cried Mr Elder. "It would take us years to get enough food together. We need to call in reinforcements."

It is a fact, although not a pleasant one, that if you want delicious food and lots of it, you need to find an ogre. In this case, more than one ogre would be required.

78

"It's lucky his castle is so big," commented Elvis. "Those ogres are not going to want to cook and then disappear. They'll have to be invited."

As the guest list grew, so did Giant Jeremiah's plans.

"I've wired up the castle with five thousand little lights," he grinned. "They flicker a bit but they look festive. And I'm going to floodlight the castle, too."

"I dare not set foot in that place unless someone has checked out the electrical system," said one anxious elf.

Now, elves are clever with most things, but a giant's castle is BIG, and elves are very small. When there is technical work to be done, sadly, you need trolls. Twenty sensible trolls were invited to check out the giant's handiwork and set up a sound system that would make Elvis's music loud enough for giant ears.

At last the great day arrived — and so did another thirty trolls, twenty-three gatecrashing ogres and another large contingent of giants. The castle, lit up like a beacon in rainbow shades of laser lighting, positively pulsated with the music and the stomping of several hundred huge feet. It was definitely an earthshaking event.

I am also happy to report that there were no elfin casualties, except for two of Mrs Elder's nephews who ate too much pie and needed a day in bed to recover.

If you're ever invited to a giant's party, don't hesitate to accept — as long as you know there will be ogres and trolls and elves there as well, of course.